That

CROWS
HATE PeoPLe!

And other Strange facts

GARY SPROTT

Rourke
Educational Media
rourkeeducationalmedia.com

A Division of
Carson Dellosa
Education

BEFORE AND DURING READING ACTIVITIES

Before Reading: *Building Background Knowledge and Vocabulary*

Building background knowledge can help children process new information and build upon what they already know. Before reading a book, it is important to tap into what children already know about the topic. This will help them develop their vocabulary and increase their reading comprehension.

Questions and Activities to Build Background Knowledge:

1. Look at the front cover of the book and read the title. What do you think this book will be about?
2. What do you already know about this topic?
3. Take a book walk and skim the pages. Look at the table of contents, photographs, captions, and bold words. Did these text features give you any information or predictions about what you will read in this book?

Vocabulary: *Vocabulary Is Key to Reading Comprehension*

Use the following directions to prompt a conversation about each word.

- Read the vocabulary words.
- What comes to mind when you see each word?
- What do you think each word means?

> **Vocabulary Words:**
> - avian
> - raptors
> - fertilize
> - ruffle
> - native
> - wary

During Reading: *Reading for Meaning and Understanding*

To achieve deep comprehension of a book, children are encouraged to use close reading strategies. During reading, it is important to have children stop and make connections. These connections result in deeper analysis and understanding of a book.

 Close Reading a Text

During reading, have children stop and talk about the following:

- Any confusing parts
- Any unknown words
- Text to text, text to self, text to world connections
- The main idea in each chapter or heading

Encourage children to use context clues to determine the meaning of any unknown words. These strategies will help children learn to analyze the text more thoroughly as they read.

When you are finished reading this book, turn to the next-to-last page for **After Reading Questions** and an **Activity**.

Table of Contents

Bird Brain Power!

A bird's brain can be as teensy as a peanut. But don't call these feathered flappers birdbrains! They are winged wonders of nature—fast, fearless, and full of surprises.

The Family Tree

Birds most likely evolved from two-legged dinosaurs. Those ancestors included the ferocious *Tyrannosaurus rex*. Yikes, that big guy would need a lot of birdseed!

Better think twice before you scare off a crow and **ruffle** its feathers. These birds can recognize humans. They learn to dislike those who treat them badly. You could say they never forget a face!

 **ruffle** (RUHF-uhl): to fluff up or disturb; also to make someone feel annoyed, worried, or unsettled

If the owl and the pussycat really did go to sea, well, the owl would probably be the lookout. These wise guys have eyes that work like binoculars and can spot prey over great distances. "Mouse, ahoy!"

Isn't There a Shortcut?

Arctic terns migrate each year between Greenland and Antarctica. That's a twisty trip of 44,000 miles (71,000 kilometers). Not bad for a bird that weighs less than the book in your hands!

With a brain that works like yours, parrots are the straight-A students of the **avian** family. They can talk and—get this—understand math! No wonder pirates with treasure to count keep parrots on their shoulders

Little Drummer Bird

On the Pacific island of New Guinea, male palm cockatoos make music to impress the girls. These crested parrots use seedpods and twigs like drumsticks to bang out rhythms on hollow trees. "May I have this—squawk!—dance?"

avian (AY-vee-uhn): related to birds

When it's time for the cuckoo to start a family, this cheeky bird drops in as an unwanted guest. Cuckoos lay their eggs in the nests of other birds. The foster family cares for the egg until it hatches. Then, it raises the impostor chick. Now that's cuckoo!

But Mom, I Want My Own Room!

After hatching, common cuckoos heave the eggs or chicks of their host family out of the nest. "Sorry, just trying to spread my wings here."

A Eurasian reed warbler feeds a common cuckoo.

On the Ground

Not every bird is ready for takeoff. The ostrich can't fly, but other birds still look up to this **native** of Africa. Stretching up to nine feet (three meters) tall and weighing as much as 300 pounds (136 kilograms), it's no surprise that the world's biggest bird can't get off the ground.

 native (NAY-tiv): a person, animal, or plant that originally lived or grew in a certain place

Big Bird? What Big Bird?

It's hard to hide when you're as tall as some elephants. So, when in danger, the ostrich blends into its sandy surroundings by laying its long neck along the ground. But, no, it doesn't actually bury its head in the sand.

Be very **wary** around the cassowary. Its nickn
is *murderbird*!

Found in Australia, these massive creatures
are like ninja warriors with an attitude. They can
run 30 miles (48 kilometers) per hour, jump
five feet (1.5 meters) in the air, and have a
five-inch (13-centimeter) claw on the middle toe
of each foot! Oh, yeah, they also have a helmet
made of keratin. That's the same stuff your
fingernails are made of.

wary (WAIR-ee): cautious and careful

Why fly like a bird when you can swim like a fish? Penguins spend most of their lives in the ocean. They flap their stubby wings to zip through the water at up to six miles (ten kilometers) per hour.

Excuse Me, Is This Spot Taken?

When they do waddle ashore, penguins huddle together in rookeries of as many as one million pairs. During breeding season, the male emperor penguin moves around with his mate's egg resting on the top of his feet.

Feathered Friends

Falcons, hawks, and other **raptors** have been used to hunt for thousands of years. Sometimes called the sport of kings, falconry involves training birds of prey to catch other birds, hares, and rabbits.

Dive Bombers

Peregrine falcons are the fastest creatures on the planet. These swift assassins can reach speeds of 240 miles (386 kilometers) per hour during their dives. That's as fast as a Formula One race car.

raptors (RAP-tuhrz): birds that hunt animals for food

Bird poop is nothing to sniff at! In the 19th century, guano was big business. Ships sailed around the world to collect the droppings of seabirds such as pelicans and blue-footed boobies. Yes, we said it, boobies. The guano was used to **fertilize** crops that helped feed America's growing population.

 fertilize (FUR-tuh-lize): to put a substance such as manure on land to make it richer and to help crops grow better

Did you know that pigeons helped save thousands of lives during World War I?

The birds flew through cannon fire to deliver vital messages to troops and spies and to carry blood supplies to hospitals. Legendary carrier pigeon Cher Ami lost a leg after being shot and was awarded a military medal for heroism!

I Hear Home!

Scientists believe that homing pigeons use low-frequency sound waves to map their way home. It's as if the birds hear directions bouncing up from the ground below them.

Don't get a gander's dander up. Geese have excellent eyesight and hearing. They protect their territory bravely—and loudly. That's why these waterfowl are used to guard chicken flocks and, in some parts of China, police stations. "Honk-honk!"

Clearing the Runway

Geese pose a deadly risk to aircraft. Every year, thousands of bird collisions cause damage, emergency landings, and, sometimes, crashes. At some airports, predatory birds such as eagles are trained to scare away geese and other nuisance flocks.

During the 20th century, coal miners carried an unusual companion with them underground: a canary. The little yellow songbird is more sensitive than humans to toxic gases such as carbon monoxide. If the caged canary became ill, the miners knew it was time to get out of the coal mine.

Memory Game

Look at the pictures. What do you remember reading on the pages where each image appeared?